ABEL AND THE WOLF

By Sergio Lairla

Illustrated by Alessandra Roberti

Translated by Marianne Martens

NORTH-SOUTH BOOKS · NEW YORK · LONDON

Abel had lived with his parents for many years, but he was now grown up. It was time for him to make his own way in the world. Before he left, his father gave him a walking stick, a knife, and a large pot. His mother gave him some herbs, seeds, and a book with golden letters. "This belonged to your grandfather," she told him as she wrapped it in a cloth. "Now it will be yours."

After the three embraced, Abel started his journey. He knew that his parents would always be in his heart, no matter how far he roamed.

Abel walked for many days until he reached a dark forest. He decided to settle there. This forest, however, belonged to a wolf, as many forests do.

Before long Abel came to a clearing beside a brook whose
bubbling song reminded him of his mother's voice, so that is
where he decided to build his house. Abel worked for many
days and many nights. The wolf watched his every move,
jealous of the lovely new house and angered by Abel's
intrusion into *his* woods.

    The wolf kept watch as Abel finished his house, cleared the land, and planted crops.

    Weeks passed and one morning the wolf smelled a wonderful aroma coming from Abel's kitchen. The wolf's mouth began to water. When he saw Abel head off to get a drink from the spring, the wolf slipped, quick as a flash, into the house and snatched the meal from Abel's pot.

Back in his den, the wolf quickly devoured the meal. He had never tasted anything so delicious.

"Ha!" laughed the wolf. "This will teach him to move into *my* forest. He may be hardworking, but I am much more clever!"

But Abel wasn't discouraged. He just flipped through the pages in his book, grabbed his pot, and started to prepare a new meal.

That made the wolf angry. "He thinks he has everything he needs," he scoffed as he looked at Abel's garden. "But it's all mine—the whole forest belongs to me."

While Abel was busy in his kitchen, the wolf ran to the garden and pulled out every plant that he could carry. Back in his den, he gobbled them up, but they didn't taste nearly as good as the meal he'd stolen from Abel.

He must be a magician, thought the wolf. That is why his food tastes so good. I bet it has something to do with his special pot and golden book.

The wolf crept up to Abel's house once again and peeked in the window to see if he could find out Abel's secret. Instead, he saw a table set for two. "How dare he!" the wolf exclaimed. "First he invades my forest and now he is inviting others to join him!"

Furious, the wolf ran back to his den. "I should have attacked him the minute he came into this forest," he snarled. "He doesn't belong here."

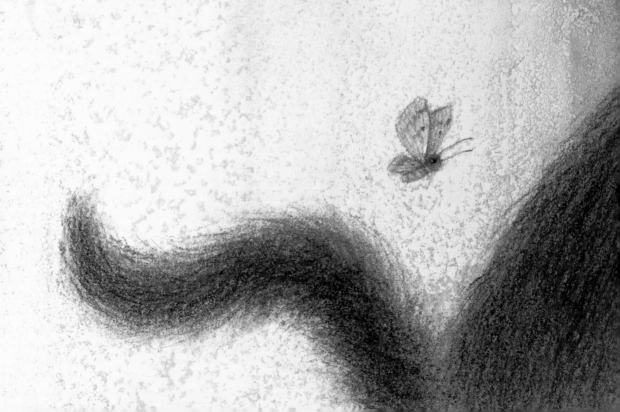

Just then, the wolf heard someone calling him.

"Hello, wolf," said Abel. "I'm Abel. I've come to invite you for dinner."

The wolf hesitated. What should he do? Aha! he thought. Now I have him! First I'll eat his food and then I'll eat him, too! The magic pot and the golden book will be mine.

The wolf entered Abel's house and started eating. Everything tasted wonderful. Abel chatted away as if he didn't have a care in the world, but the wolf didn't listen. He was just waiting for the perfect moment to attack.

When Abel went to get a bowl of strawberries, the wolf saw his chance. Now! he thought. Then he lunged!

But at that very moment, Abel bent down to pick up a towel that had fallen on the floor. The wolf flew over Abel's head and crashed into the fire. Flames shot everywhere, burning the wolf's paws. Howling in pain, he collapsed on the floor.

Abel ran to the table and grabbed the knife. The wolf was certain that Abel was going to kill him. But Abel simply began to cut the towel into strips. Then he wrapped up the wolf's paws.

"Oh, this is terrible," yelped the wolf. "I'm in so much pain."

"Don't worry," said Abel. "I'll take care of you until you are well again."

"Even though I could eat you at any moment?" asked the wolf in disbelief.

"Yes, I know you could," said Abel. "This is your forest and you are very powerful. But I have always liked seeing you outside my house. You made me feel less alone."

The wolf was strangely pleased to hear that. Of course, he didn't give up the idea of eating Abel. He just had to wait for his paws to heal.

Abel took good care of the wolf. Each day, while he was cooking, Abel would talk to the wolf and sometimes ask him to taste a new recipe. The wolf never said much, until one day he hesitantly volunteered, "Hmmm, needs a little salt." Abel smiled.

The day finally came for the wolf's bandages to come off. He stretched his paws wide. His muscles were strong and his claws were sharp. But when he looked at Abel, he couldn't bring himself to attack.

Abel wasn't an intruder anymore. He was a friend.